Presented To:

_____

From:

_____

On This Date:

_____

truth becomes her

© 2016 Bible Belles
www.truthbecomesher.com

Books may be purchased by contacting the publisher Truth Becomes Her, at hello@truthbecomesher.com

Published in San Diego, California by Truth Becomes Her. Bible Belles and Truth Becomes Her are registered trademarks.

This book was created as a result of hard work, prayers, coffee, prayers, a lot of late nights, prayers, so much help from others, prayers, and a whole bunch of God's grace. Did we mention prayers?

Illustrations by: Rob Corley and Chuck Vollmer

Interior Design by: Ron Eddy

Cover Design by: Rob Corley and Ron Eddy

Editing by: Julie Breihan

Printed in the United States

ISBN 978-0-9961689-2-2

The Adventures of Rooney Cruz

Esther
The Belle of Patience

written by
Erin Weidemann

illustrated by
Rob Corley and Chuck Vollmer

Welcome, Little Belle.

Your superhero journey
begins right now...

Rooney watched her teammates from the sideline. She liked Saturday soccer games. Even though she didn't

get to play very often, it was still fun to wear that icy blue uniform and be outside in the warm, shining sun.

Please, God, help us do our best today. And it would be really awesome if anyone other than Amanda got to touch the ball.

Suddenly, a fast-moving blur whipped past the bench.

It was Amanda.

The other girls on the field called for the ball, but Amanda either couldn't hear them or wasn't listening. With her head down, she dipped and ducked between the girls in red on her way to score another goal.

Rooney turned to her friend Daniela. "How many is that today?"

Dani shrugged. "Man, I don't know. I lost count."

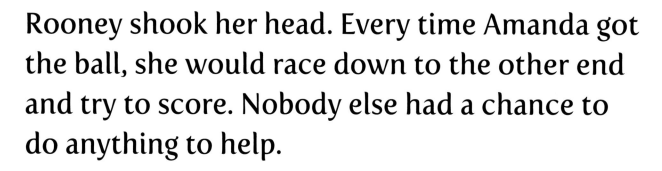

Rooney shook her head. Every time Amanda got the ball, she would race down to the other end and try to score. Nobody else had a chance to do anything to help.

"I've tried to talk to her a few times," Dani said. "She's a great player, but it's like all she cares about is herself."

"Maybe Coach can do something," Rooney said as she watched him on the sideline. *"Hey, Coach, Amanda is—"* Rooney started to say.

"Hang on,"

Dani quickly grabbed the back of Rooney's shirt. "I'm not sure now is a good time. But I get it. It'd be great if she actually let one of us play too."

"Yeah, that would be great, wouldn't it?"

Rooney whirled around. She knew that voice anywhere. "Mari, hey! You're at my game. This is so cool!"

Mari laughed as she fluttered her wings wildly. "Rooney, I always watch your games. Personal angel, hello!"

Rooney giggled. "Oh yeah."

Just then the whistle blew.

Ugh, that's it?

Rooney and Dani looked at each other.

It's over?

The referee waved, and the teams cleared the field. The girls turned around to find their water bottles. Mari zipped into the side pocket of Rooney's soccer bag.

"Ladies," Rooney heard her coach's strong voice, "pack it up and let's meet in our usual spot."

Mari poked her angel head out the side of Rooney's zipper pocket. "I'm going to hang around for a minute. I'd like to sit in on this one."

The girls walked over to the usual shady spot and sat down together in the grass. Except for Amanda.

"Ladies, another great win today. You all—"

"Thanks, Coach," Amanda interrupted. She turned to the team. "Another great game. I know I'll make All Stars for sure." Then she kneeled down and whispered in the ear of another girl.

Did he hear that? Rooney looked up. Her coach had turned and was talking to a parent. *Ugh, of course not.*

Rooney could feel hot bubbles start to burn inside her stomach. She and Dani locked eyes. *Who does she think she is?* Rooney's hand shot up.

"Hey, Coach. You know what? I'm sick of—"

"Alright, girls." Coach turned back to the team. "Great job today and we'll see you at practice. Bring it in for a cheer."

Rooney gritted her teeth as she and the other girls huddled up, put their hands in, and muttered a weak "Kangaroos" before heading off toward their families.

Mari jabbed Rooney with her little elbow. "Hey, are you up for another adventure?"

"Right now?"

"Yeah! Enough is enough. It's time for a sneak peek at another Bible Belle. You've got to see Esther in action."

"Action?"

"Yeah. Action! Like in the movies. Esther was kind of like a movie star. In fact," Mari said as she wiggled in the air, "her name means 'star.'"

"Okay." Rooney smiled.

"Let's do this." Mari held out her hand. "Can I borrow your water bottle?"

"Sure." Rooney grabbed the bottle and handed it to Mari. She popped off the cap and balanced it on her tiny finger.

The cap jumped, and then it began to spin. Round and round until BOOM! It shot straight up and exploded to reveal a wide, wooden window.

"Amazing!" Rooney climbed up into the corner and peered down at the scene below.

The beautiful palace was alive with music and dancing. Rooney could see a man with a crown on his head sitting on the throne, but he did not look happy.

"What do you mean the queen isn't coming?" Rooney heard the king, his voice sizzling with anger.

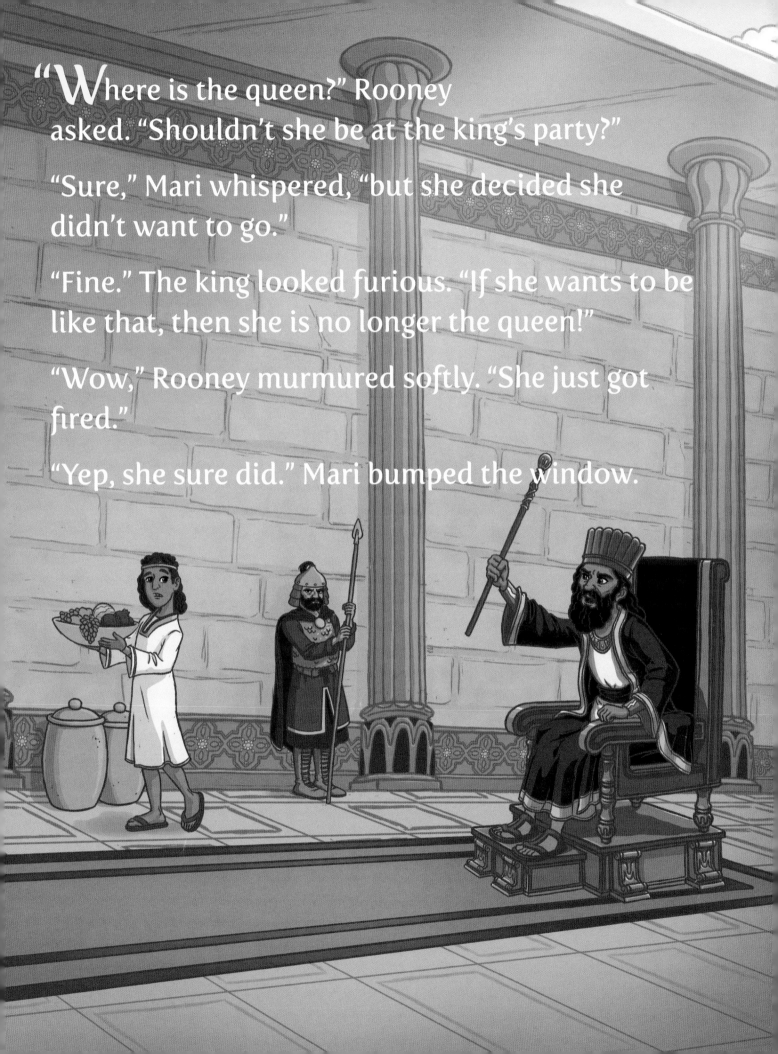

"Where is the queen?" Rooney asked. "Shouldn't she be at the king's party?"

"Sure," Mari whispered, "but she decided she didn't want to go."

"Fine." The king looked furious. "If she wants to be like that, then she is no longer the queen!"

"Wow," Rooney murmured softly. "She just got fired."

"Yep, she sure did." Mari bumped the window.

It bounced, and Rooney saw two people walking slowly toward the enormous gates of the palace.

"Wait," Rooney said. *"Is that Esther?* She does kind of remind me of a movie star. Mari, is she the new queen?"

Mari nodded. "Her cousin Mordecai is taking her inside. She was chosen out of thousands of others to be the queen, and," Mari giggled, "you're about to find out why."

"I love you, my cousin," Rooney heard Esther say. "Thank you for being with me."

"Don't worry, my dear." Mordecai hugged her. "No matter where you are, you are loved and protected."

Rooney put her head down. *God, please be with Esther. She probably doesn't know anyone in there, and she might be scared. Please keep her safe.*

"Hey, Mari," Rooney whispered, "when we went to see Hannah, you said all of the Bible Belles have superpowers. What's Esther's?"

Mari grinned. "You'll have to wait to find that out." Mari clapped, and the window revealed a new scene.

Crowds of people were crouched low as a man walked through the king's gate, but Esther's cousin Mordecai was on his feet.

"Who's that?" Rooney asked.

"That's Haman," Mari explained. "He's the king's second in command."

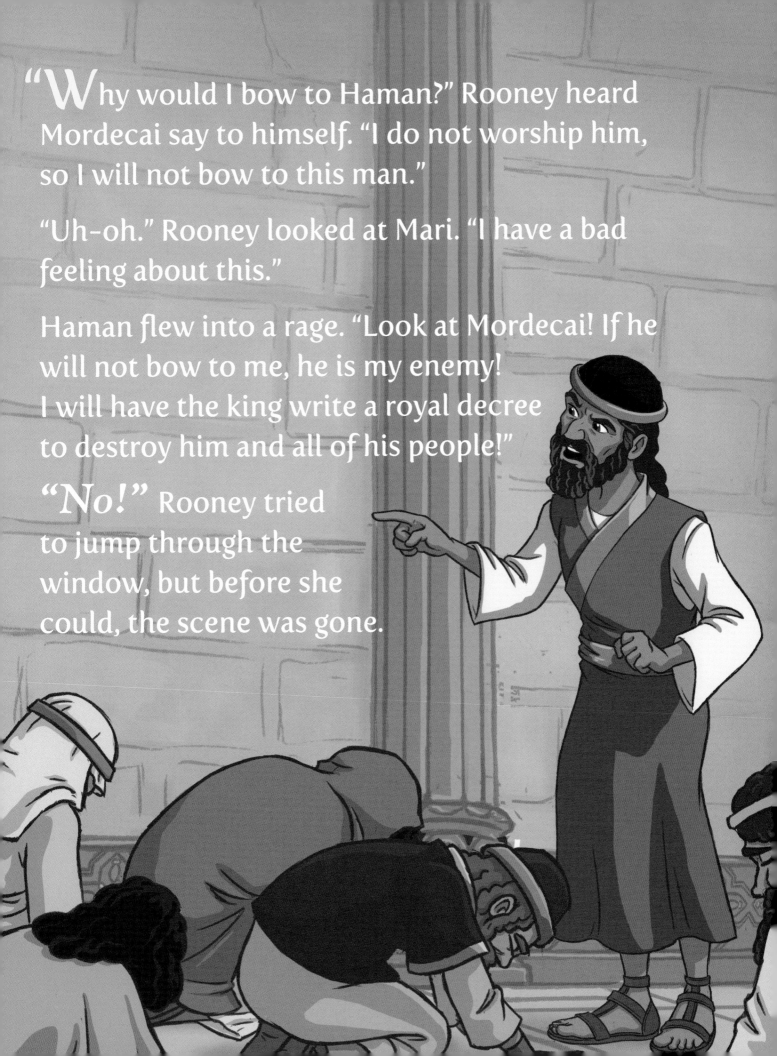

"Why would I bow to Haman?" Rooney heard Mordecai say to himself. "I do not worship him, so I will not bow to this man."

"Uh-oh." Rooney looked at Mari. "I have a bad feeling about this."

Haman flew into a rage. "Look at Mordecai! If he will not bow to me, he is my enemy! I will have the king write a royal decree to destroy him and all of his people!"

"*No!*" Rooney tried to jump through the window, but before she could, the scene was gone.

Now Rooney could see Mordecai. He was crying. He had ripped his clothes, and Esther was trying to comfort him.

"Esther, please," Mordecai begged. "We're in trouble. All of us. Even you. You have to talk to the king. You have to tell him to save our people!"

"How?" Esther asked. "How can I talk to him? I'm not allowed to go see the king unless he calls for me. If I try to speak to him without being summoned, it might make him angry. I'm not even sure what to say."

"If you don't do this," Mordecai lowered his voice, "our people will surely be saved another way, but you and your family may not survive." Mordecai kneeled down next to his cousin.

"Who knows?" he whispered. *"Maybe this is exactly why you were chosen to be the queen.* It's the perfect time for you to be here. I think you are the one who is supposed to do this."

Esther stood up. "Alright, I will go and talk to the king, but I have to make sure I do it at the right time."

"Mari," Rooney was confused. "How is she supposed to know when it's the right time to talk to the king?"

"Well, Esther knows what she needs to do," Mari explained, "but she decides to pray about what she is going to say and when she should approach the king. She does this for three days."

"*She waits three days?* That must have seemed like forever."

Mari nodded in agreement. " On the third day, she asks the king to come to a feast that she has prepared. Take a look."

Rooney peered down through the window again. She could see Esther standing before the king. Haman was there too.

"Mari!" Rooney cried. "What's happening? Why is Haman at Esther's feast?"

"It's okay, Rooney," Mari said. "Esther invited him too."

"Queen Esther," the king gently held the queen's hand, "what is your request? I'll give you anything. Even up to half my kingdom."

"My king, I hope that you are pleased with me and that you would grant my request. Would you and Haman come to another feast tomorrow? Then I will say what I have to say."

"Mari." Rooney was confused. "*Why doesn't she just ask him now?*"

"Well, she's waiting." Mari smiled. "Maybe she knows something that we don't."

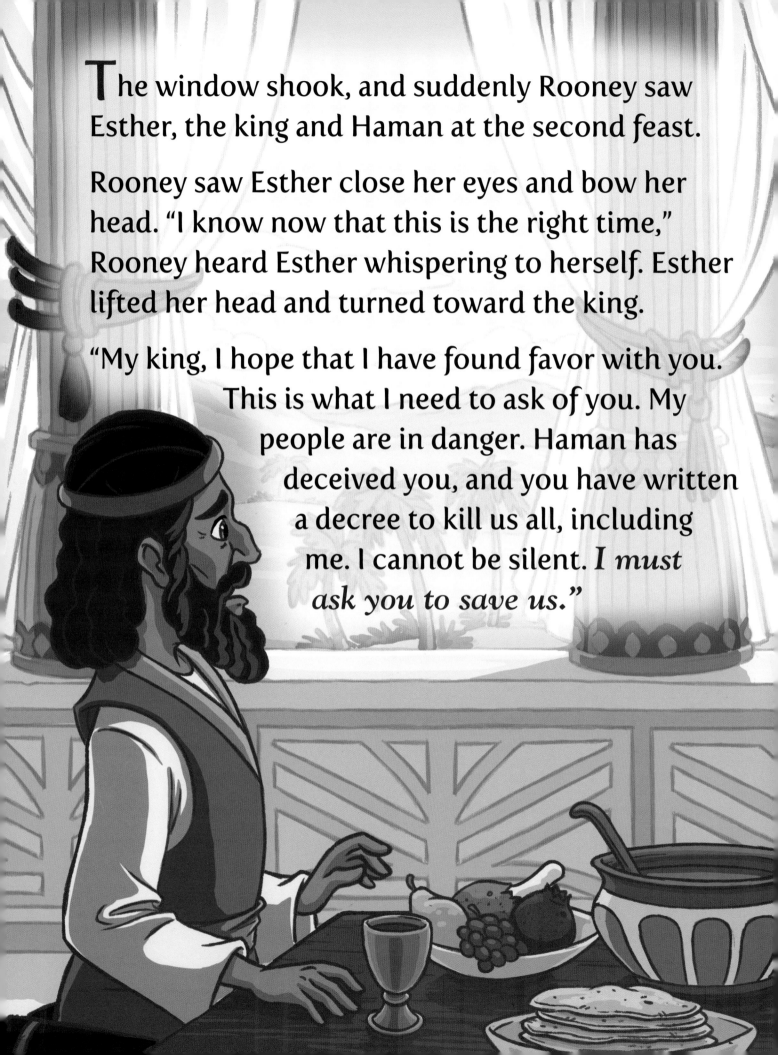

The window shook, and suddenly Rooney saw Esther, the king and Haman at the second feast.

Rooney saw Esther close her eyes and bow her head. "I know now that this is the right time," Rooney heard Esther whispering to herself. Esther lifted her head and turned toward the king.

"My king, I hope that I have found favor with you. This is what I need to ask of you. My people are in danger. Haman has deceived you, and you have written a decree to kill us all, including me. I cannot be silent. *I must ask you to save us.*"

The king was furious. "Haman, what have you done? You are a terrible enemy to me and to my queen! Esther, I will save you and your people from this man's evil plan!"

"Yes!"

Rooney jumped into the air. "She did it!"

"I know!" Mari said. "Esther saved her people because she was patient. She waited and listened for God's voice to guide her until it was the right time for her to speak up."

"Wow!"

Just then Rooney felt a warm wave come over her. "Mari, I know I can talk to God and that He will always hear me. I've tried talking to my Coach about the problem with Amanda, but I see now that it wasn't the right time. Will God help me be patient like He helped Esther?"

Mari smiled. "*Yes, He will.* Listen, I know you're upset about what's going on. Talking to an adult can be a little scary sometimes, but something is wrong and the team needs your help. Pray about it first, and let God speak to you."

"But, Mari, how will I know what to do?"

"Remember," Mari patted Rooney's hand, "Esther prepared for what she had to do. She spent time praying and listening for God's voice, and she waited patiently for just the right moment. *You can do it too. I know you can.*"

"Okay, Mari. I'll give it a try."

Rooney sat down gently and bowed her head.

"Dear God, I know I need to talk to my coach. Even though I'm scared, I trust that You're guiding me and I know You will protect me. Please talk to me. I am listening for You. Tell me the words You want me to say. Please help me be brave. I want to be respectful and kind to my coach. Please help me know the right time to talk to him. I want to show him I care about all of my teammates, even Amanda."

Rooney looked across the field. She saw her coach sitting under a tree alone, writing something on his clipboard.

"Mari," Rooney said, "I think now might be a good time."

"You got this."

Rooney walked toward her coach, praying all the way.

After several minutes, Rooney came back over to Mari.

"So," Mari said gently, "how'd it go?"

"I told him that I love being on the team, and that I'm feeling a little sad about some of the things Amanda said earlier. I want us all to work together and to be kind to each other, so I asked him if he could help us do that a little better."

"See?" Mari nudged her, grinning. *"You did it!* It wasn't so hard. Remember, God is always with you and He will always help you. He can hear your voice, and you can hear His voice too. All you have to do is pray and listen for Him. He will tell you what to do and when to do it. Just stay faithful and be ready for Him to lead you. *Way to 'wait!'"*

"You know what happens now."

Mari spun her hands around, and a bright, shining bell appeared. The bell glowed brightly, reflecting the light from the afternoon sun.

"Whoa!"

Mari held out her hands.
"Rooney, this is the Bell of Patience. It will help you
remember the power you have to wait and trust
God's timing. He promises that He will give you the
direction you need. Keep listening for Him, wait
faithfully, and He will guide you."

Rooney jumped up. "Two bells, Prayer and Patience! I'm a real superhero, just like Hannah and Esther! I can't believe it. Thanks, Mari!"

"No problem." Mari winked. "Don't forget, the more you use your powers, the stronger they get."

"I won't forget!" Rooney smiled and tucked the shimmering bell inside her soccer bag. She ran over to Dani, her stomach dancing with tiny pings of excitement.

She had a feeling that something big was about to happen.

I wait for the LORD, my whole being waits, and in His word I put my hope.

— Psalm 130:5

Check our website for free resources,
products and more books from
The Adventures of Rooney Cruz series.

truthbecomesher.com